THE SALAMANDER AND THE SEA

A story about love, freedom and the courage to choose who we are

BETZABETH JARAMILLO

Publication and Distribution
The Salamander and the Sea
By Betzabeth Jaramillo Hurtado

First Edition, 2024.
ISBN: 978-1-0691877-2-7
Save Creative Registration:
2412160391283

To You, Dear Reader

If you're reading these words, it means this book has found its way to you, and that means the world to me. Thanks to platforms like Amazon, I've been able to share this story with you, carefully tending to every detail—from the writing to the editing and formatting. While I've poured my heart into this work, I acknowledge that there might be a small error here or there; if so, I kindly ask for your understanding.

Your opinion means so much. If this story has touched or inspired you, I would be incredibly grateful if you could leave a review on Amazon. That simple gesture helps others discover this book and its message.

I hope these pages leave left a mark on your heart, because that is the greatest gift for a writer: to know their words and to have found someone special.

With all my gratitude,

Betzabeth Jaramillo

Legal Notice and Reserved Rights

To Mily, for holding me up and enduring me, even when the weight of my world seemed unsustainable.

To Alonso, for reminding me of the magic of life.

And to Autana, for helping me find the words and being the unexpected light that guided this dream into reality.

To those who love with all their hearts, yet never forget who they are.

To those who find strength in their differences, the strength to return, again and again, without losing themselves.

And above all, to those who, like the salamander, shine even in the depths.

"To shine in the depths is an act of love."

TABLE OF CONTENTS

Feel every word is alive in this story

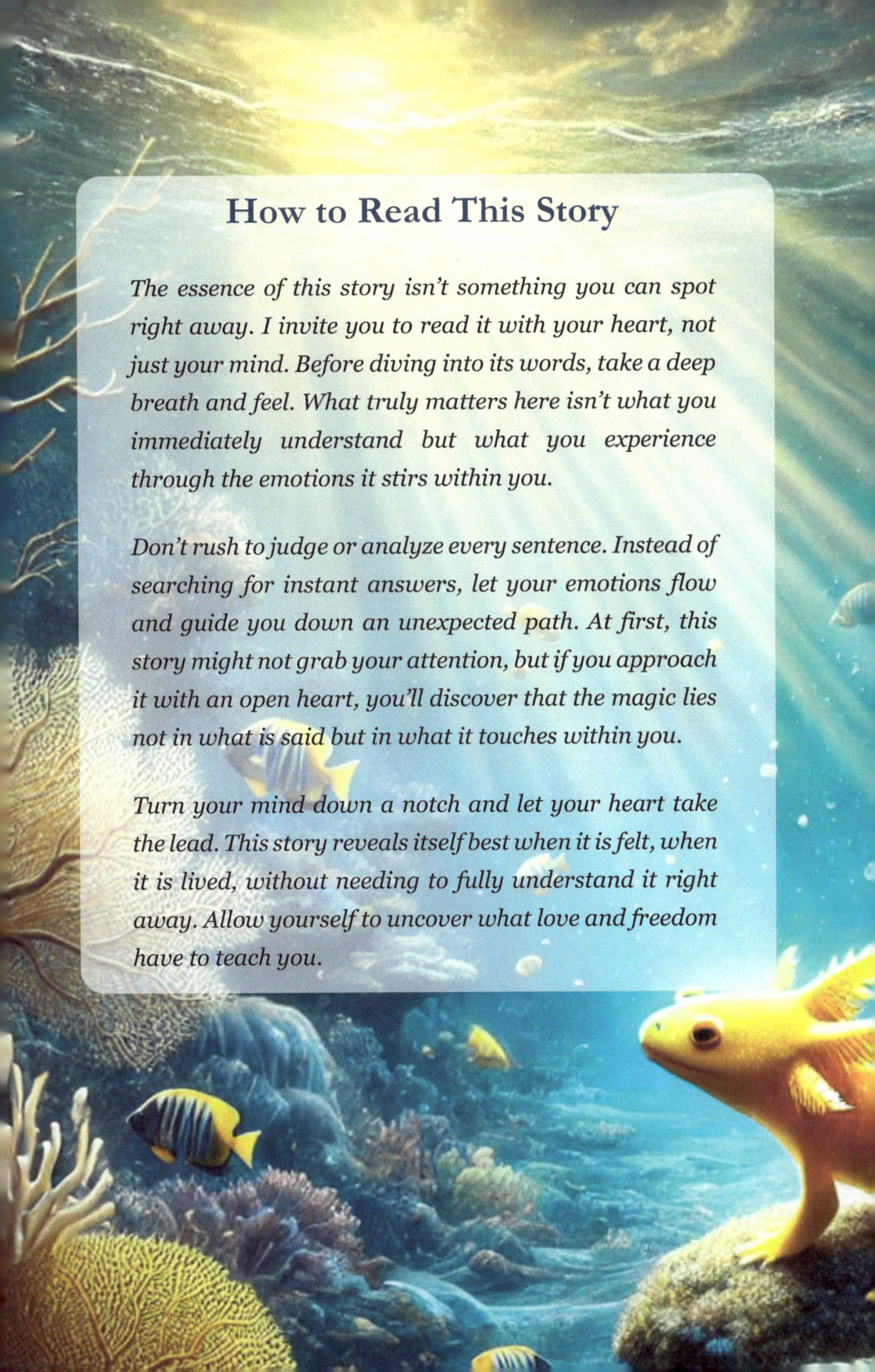

How to Read This Story

The essence of this story isn't something you can spot right away. I invite you to read it with your heart, not just your mind. Before diving into its words, take a deep breath and feel. What truly matters here isn't what you immediately understand but what you experience through the emotions it stirs within you.

Don't rush to judge or analyze every sentence. Instead of searching for instant answers, let your emotions flow and guide you down an unexpected path. At first, this story might not grab your attention, but if you approach it with an open heart, you'll discover that the magic lies not in what is said but in what it touches within you.

Turn your mind down a notch and let your heart take the lead. This story reveals itself best when it is felt, when it is lived, without needing to fully understand it right away. Allow yourself to uncover what love and freedom have to teach you.

A Short Introduction

There are stories, brief as they may be, that stay with us forever. The Salamander and the Sea is one of those. It's not just a tale—it's an invitation to see with the eyes of the heart, to dive into the depths of love and freedom, and to discover how much we can learn from the tides within ourselves.

In these few pages, you'll find more than words; you'll find a reflection of our own doubts, of those moments when love challenges us, transforms us, and at times, seeks to overtake or catch up with us. Because loving doesn't mean giving up who we are—it means learning to be who we are while sharing our light with others.

This story may not offer definitive answers, but in its simplicity and honesty, it might guide you toward an essential truth: love is not just something we feel; it's something we show. And in every act of love, there is also an act of being true to ourselves.

If you've ever felt that love drowns you, demands more than you can give, or if you've wondered how to love without losing yourself, this story is for you. Let the words of the salamander and the sea guide you. Perhaps, in their waves and light, you'll find a piece of yourself.

Because love, in the end, isn't about possessing or catching up. It's about seeing, accepting, and choosing another—again and again— while finding the freedom to be exactly who we are.

Between these pages, a sea of words
waits for you to dive in.

THE SALAMANDER AND THE SEA

Once upon a time, there was a salamander who fell in love with the sea, and the sea, vast and powerful, loved her back. They loved each other deeply. The salamander, small and delicate, learned to hold her breath to dive into the depths and be with her sea, for she loved it with every part of her being.

But as she swam in its waters, the salamander couldn't help but notice how her chest tightened and her breath ran thin. To be there, she had to risk her very life, and though the sea was immense and beautiful, it didn't seem to realize the sacrifice it took for her to stay within its embrace.

From time to time, the salamander had to return to the surface, to her own world. In those brief moments away, she rediscovered the softness of air filling her lungs, the warmth of the sun on her skin, the blue sky, and the stars that invited her to dream. She saw other salamanders and remembered who she was outside the water. But every breath she took on land was for one reason: to return to the sea with renewed strength and fuller lungs, even if it meant stepping away for a while.

When the sea watched her leave, it grew restless, its waves rising and crashing with fury. It couldn't understand why she needed to go, and its anger shook everything around it. Sometimes, it swept everything in its path, unleashing storms that raged uncontrollably.

"Why can't you stay with me?" it roared, its deep voice echoing through the depths. The sea couldn't grasp that demanding her constant presence was suffocating her.

The salamander tried to explain, her voice calm but firm:

"I love you, but if I stay here all the time, I will lose my breath, my essence—my life. I need to leave to breathe, to remain who I am. Without that, I won't be able to return to you. Without air, I can't love anything—not even you."

But the sea, vast and proud, refused to understand. Its love was overwhelming, but also possessive. While the salamander risked everything to be with it, the sea sought to consume all of her, blind to the lengths she went to just to stay by its side.

The salamander's light beneath the water captivated the fish, who swam closer in awe. Other creatures, too, were drawn to her glow, marveling at her uniqueness and beauty. This only deepened the sea's jealousy, unable to see that while others admired her, the salamander's love wasn't something she shared romantically—it belonged to the sea alone.

She loved everyone, but the one she would give her very last breath to was the sea.

Yet fear began to grow in the heart of the sea. Fear of losing her. Fear that, on one of her ventures to the world above, she might discover something else—the sky, the sun, the trees, or perhaps even the fisherman. But what the sea feared most was that, in the salamander's way of loving the whole world, she might fall in love with someone else. With a fish, or maybe even with the writer of this story.

And one day, it happened. From its depths, the sea saw the salamander speaking with a fish. It wasn't the same as her; they didn't share the same world, they didn't seek the same things, they didn't even eat the same food. But there they were, sharing a moment. Just talking. And the sea felt a pain it had never known before.

"What if she falls in love with him? What if she chooses him? What if she stops coming back to me?" the sea wondered, its waves heavy with doubt.

The sea feared that the salamander, in her boundless capacity to love, might look toward someone else. That, just as she had once chosen the sea, she could one day choose another—perhaps even the person reading this story.

But what the sea didn't understand was that, although the salamander loved everyone with her whole heart, her love for him was never in question.

She had chosen the sea, and only the sea, to give everything she was—even if he didn't fully realize it.

No matter the storms he caused or his struggle to understand her, the salamander always returned to his embrace. Not because she had to, but because her way of loving wasn't bound by expectations or fears. It was free, genuine, and true. She loved the world and every being within it, but she had chosen the sea as her home, her refuge, and her greatest love.

She knew that to keep loving him as deeply as she did, she needed to leave his waters from time to time. She had to find herself, to breathe, to reconnect with the air, the sky, and her soul. Only then, with her heart full and her spirit grounded, could she return to him—return to his endless waves and wrap herself in his vastness once more.

As the years passed, the salamander began to adapt to the world beneath the surface. Out of her devotion to the sea and her desire to stay by his side, she trained her body to hold her breath for longer and longer. At first, it was for months; then, for years. Her capacity to hold oxygen grew with every return, until she could spend two, three, even six years in his embrace without needing to surface. And every time she did return to his arms, it was with the same love, the same light, and the same quiet promise she had made from the start: You are my choice, always.

Even with her growing adaptation to the depths, the salamander knew she would one day have to return to the surface.

No matter how long she could remain beneath the waves, she could never fully give up who she was. Those rare escapes—though less frequent—were vital, not only for her survival but also as a reminder that she was much more than her love for the sea.

And the sea, vast and watchful, would notice. In quiet moments, when no one else could see, the sea observed its beloved with awe. He saw the salamander shine beneath the water, her light drawing creatures of all kinds toward her. He understood why they were captivated; her brilliance was her essence, something that could neither be dimmed nor contained. Yet, even as he admired her, this same light stirred his insecurities.

The sea couldn't silence the question that haunted him: What if she realizes she doesn't need me? Or worse, What if her love for the stars, the sun, or the trees takes her away from me forever? These fears would churn within him, and at times, they spilled over into storms.

But the salamander saw the sea more clearly than he realized. She understood his vastness, but also the quiet tremors of doubt that rippled through him. Her love for him was constant, yet she knew it didn't mean forsaking the rest of the world. For the salamander, to love the sea was also to love all that surrounded him—the fish that swam within his waters, the waves that kissed the shore, and every place where the sea touched life itself.

In her heart, she knew that loving the sea was not about choosing one thing over another. It was about seeing the beauty in everything he connected to, and in turn, remaining true to herself.

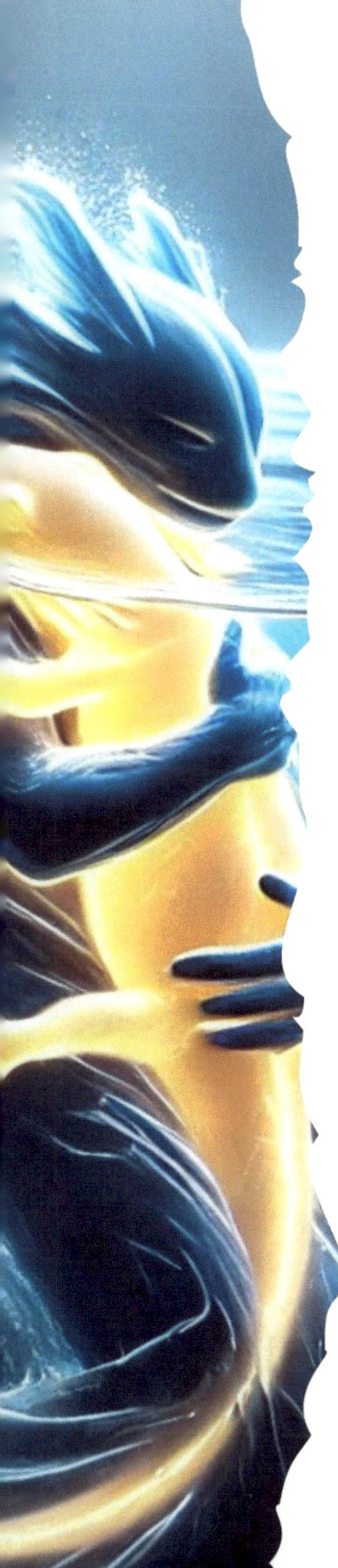

One day the sea, in its vastness, couldn't hold back its longing and asked the salamander:

— "Why can't you be like me? If you truly loved me, you wouldn't need to return to the surface. You would stay here, with me, in my depths, where I can keep everything under control."

The salamander, glowing with her light and essence of freedom, looked at him with quiet understanding. She wasn't vast or constant like the sea. She was something entirely different, and in her difference lay her truth.

— "I don't love you because you're like me," she replied, her voice steady. "I love you because you're everything I'm not. And you love me for who I am. My freedom doesn't take me away from you—it's what lets me come back."

The sea rumbled softly, its waves rippling with uncertainty. His love was overwhelming, always seeking to hold, to encompass, to possess. But the salamander was unlike anything else in his waters.

— "Maybe what you love most about me," she added gently, "is the very thing you cannot control: that I am free."

The sea, vast and eternal, fell into silence.

That night, as the salamander rested under the stars, her thoughts drifted to love.

"To love isn't to possess," she thought. "To love is to let the other be free and still choose to stay."

Her love for the sea was unwavering, but she also knew that her light—her very essence—was a gift she could never surrender, not even for him.

And so, she looked at the stars, her thoughts quiet, while the sea remained below, its waves softly reaching toward the shore.

Perhaps some might question the way the salamander loved the sea. They might think her love wasn't enough because she couldn't always remain in his arms. But if we look beyond her words and thoughts, if we focus on her actions, we'll see the truth of her love: she held air in her lungs, risked her very life, and still returned to him, again and again.

The salamander didn't love through promises or grand declarations. Her love lived in every breath she saved to return, in every choice she made to come back to the sea, and in every moment they shared, no matter how difficult it was. For her, love was about being present—even when she couldn't stay forever.

Love doesn't reside in what we think or say; it lives in what we do. If we observe the salamander's actions—her sacrifice, her patience, her constancy—we'll know that her love for the sea was real. Because love isn't always perfect. It takes many forms, but it's always true when it is chosen, day after day.

For now, the salamander continues to swim between two worlds, loving the sea, loving herself, and facing the waves of the unknown. For now, this story continues his writing every day, floating between the waves of the sea and the breaths of the salamander.

We don't yet know how this tale will end. Will the sea ever understand all that the salamander has done for him? Will the salamander decide one day to leave forever? Perhaps she will one day lose her breath, fading away in the arms of the sea she loved so deeply.

Or maybe, one day, the salamander will learn to breathe underwater. Perhaps that would resolve everything, allowing her and the sea to be together without conflict. But would that truly be a solution? Or would it mean losing the very essence of who she is?

And in another twist of this story, perhaps the sea will choose to love another creature—one who can stay with him forever.

An Especial Gift for You, Dear Readers:

This poem, *Day by Day*, is exclusively available in the English version of *The Salamander and the Sea.*

Day by Day Poem

Day by day,
love rises like the tide,
pulling me closer,
whispering its endless waves,
yet leaving space for the shore to breathe.

Day by day,
I choose to return,
not because I must,
but because my heart knows the way
back to the vastness I adore.

In your depths, I find silence;
in my lungs, I carry air.
Together, we balance the impossible—
freedom and belonging,
two worlds colliding,
yet never breaking.

Love is not chains;
it is the courage to stay,
even when leaving is easier.
Love is, most certainly, choosing.

Final Reflection

Love is not always perfect. Sometimes, it is mistaken for the need to control, to protect, or to hold on too tightly. The sea loved the salamander with all its vastness, but in its immensity, it failed to understand that true love also requires letting the other be— letting them go, letting them breathe. The sea, despite all its power, was afraid of losing her. But what it didn't realize was that love is not about possession; it's about the freedom to choose to return, to choose to love oneself and the other as equals.

The salamander, however, understood that love doesn't mean giving up who you are or losing yourself in someone else. To love is to give your best, but also to recognize that true love allows for growth in freedom, even in the face of life's most challenging moments.

The sea, though fearful and filled with insecurities, loved deeply. Its storms were not acts of malice, but reflections of its fear of losing what it cherished most. Just as the salamander adapted, the sea, in its grandeur, needed to learn to love without chains, to respect the space of the other, and to trust in love without needing to control everything.

True love—the kind that endures—is built on the acceptance of differences, the freedom to be who we are, and mutual respect. Sometimes, to love means learning to let go while still choosing to stay. It is a cycle of giving and receiving, of teaching and learning, of growing together while remaining free as individuals.

This reflection reveals to us that both the sea and the salamander carry their vulnerabilities. In the end, love is about finding balance—with freedom, understanding, and the courage to let each other grow.

Epilogue

Love, like the sea and the salamander, is a constant journey between who we are and what we wish to share with others. This story has no end, because love never stops; it is always in motion—growing, transforming, adapting. Perhaps, somewhere in the world, you too are a salamander. Or perhaps you are the sea. This tale does not seek to provide answers, but rather to invite you to feel, to reflect, and to look within yourself to understand how you choose to love.

And so, the story of the salamander and the sea continues, not only in these pages but in every life it touches. Because to love is not an act to be completed; it is a path we walk, day after day, through all the storms and still waters it brings. For now, the salamander keeps swimming, the sea keeps loving, and you, dear reader, can write the next chapter in your own heart.

Love in Its Freest Form: Reflections on Freedom and the Human Heart

- Words from the Author-

This story is entirely fictional. It is not based on real events or specific people. Instead, it is a creative representation of love, freedom, and emotional transformation.

It's important to understand that this is not a tale of "good" or "bad" characters, but of beings who embody the complexity of human relationships. We are all sentient beings, filled with emotions, doubts, and desires. Love is a choice we make each day, with its challenges and sacrifices, and it is never static—it is always evolving.

There are no culprits or villains here, only beings who, like all of us, are trying to understand love and freedom in their own way. To love is to allow the other to be free, even when it makes us feel vulnerable. There is no malice in this story, only individuals seeking to find themselves through their unique ways of loving.

This story remains open, because we are all still writing the ways in which we love. Take from it what resonates with you, but I invite you to read it with your heart, to truly grasp its lesson.

Betzabeth Jaramillo

About the Author

Betzabeth Jaramillo is a political scientist, writer, and human rights activist. Her life and work are deeply intertwined with her commitment to freedom, justice, and protecting those who seek new horizons. Through her efforts, she has touched countless lives, offering hope and guidance to those facing migratory and social challenges.

As a writer, Betzabeth has delved into narrative and poetry, with several of her poems published in migratory fanzines, where she captures the emotions, aspirations, and resilience of those navigating change. Her sensitivity and unique style invite readers to reflect on the many forms of love, freedom, and human connection.

The Salamander and the Sea is a modern fable that embodies her profound reflections on freedom, love, and the daily choice to be authentic. Written with the heart of someone who believes that to love is an act of freedom and constancy, this story aims to inspire readers to explore the vast possibilities of love and humanity.

Puedes contactar a Betzabeth en sus redes sociales:

Instagram: @BetzabethJ

Twitter (ahora X): @Betzaj

Betzabethj.com

About the Images

This book combines text with images generated with the support of artificial intelligence, crafted from my thoughts and emotions. Each image is a visual representation of what the words seek to convey, carefully designed to complement and deepen the reading experience. These images have also been edited using design programs like Photoshop, Illustrator, and Canva to enhance the results, ensuring they align with the imagination of the author.

Like the salamander and the sea, this book is the product of an encounter between two worlds: the human and the technological. The words born from my heart intertwine with the images created through artificial intelligence, demonstrating that creativity, when combined with intention and love, can transcend boundaries. This process does not replace the human essence—it expands it, allowing us to explore new forms of expression and connection.

Just as the salamander shines in the depths, this book seeks to show that even the most unexpected tools can help us reflect the light we carry within. It is a reminder that love and creativity know no limits, and that together, humans and technology can bring stories to life that touch the heart.

Acknowledgment to the Reader

To every reader who has reached this point: thank you. This story is as much yours as it is mine, because stories come alive in those who read them. I hope this little tale has illuminated a part of your being and that its words find a home in your heart.

Special Acknowledgment

To Canada, for being the refuge where my words found freedom and my dreams a safe place to bloom. From this land of maple leaves, a foreigner writes with a heart full of gratitude, feeling welcomed, secure, and capable of making possible what once seemed unattainable.

A Space for Your Own Reflections

Love and freedom mean different things to each of us, and the journey to balance them is as unique as we are. The Salamander and the Sea invites us to reflect not just on the story, but on ourselves—on the relationships, choices, and moments that define how we love and live.

This space is yours. Take a moment to breathe, to reflect, and to listen to your heart. What did the story awaken in you? How do you navigate the currents of love, freedom, and connection in your own life?

Here are some guiding questions to inspire your thoughts, but feel free to let your mind wander beyond them:

1. What does the salamander represent for you? What about the sea?

2. Have you ever felt torn between staying true to yourself and staying close to someone you love? How did you find balance—or are you still searching?

3. What does love mean to you? Is it freedom, sacrifice, presence, or something else?

4. How do you think the story would end if you were the salamander or the sea?

You can write, sketch, or simply reflect quietly. Whatever you choose, let this be a moment for yourself, a chance to explore the vastness of your own heart and the light you carry within.

Your Notes and Reflections

This section provides a deeply personal and interactive experience for readers, allowing them to connect their own stories with the themes of the book. It not only makes the book more engaging but also gives it a lasting impact, as readers can revisit their reflections over time.

Notes and Reflections